SIOBHÁN PARKINSON grew up in Galway and Donegal and now lives in Dublin with her husband; they have a grown-up son. She is an editor, translator and critic as well as a highly acclaimed writer for children of all ages, and was the first Irish Children's Laureate (from 2010 to 2012). Several of her books have won Children's Books Ireland Bisto awards, and *The Moon King* and *Something Invisible* were also IBBY Honour Books. Her first book for Frances Lincoln was the bestselling *Spellbound: Tales of Enchantment from Ancient Ireland.*

OLWYN WHELAN was a newspaper cartoonist and graphic designer before becoming a freelance illustrator. Her goal is to produce timeless books which children will treasure for life. Her previous books include *The Mermaid of Cafur* and *The Barefoot Book of Princesses*, as well as *Spellbound: Tales of Enchantment from Ancient Ireland* with Siobhán Parkinson, for Frances Lincoln Children's Books. Olwyn lives in Dublin with her husband and two children.

MAGIC!

New Fairy Tales by Irish Writers

For Gráinne – S.P.

For Megan and Ben – O.W.

JANETTA OTTER-BARRY BOOKS

Magic! Collection copyright © Siobhán Parkinson 2015
The Princess and the Other Frog copyright © Siobhán Parkinson 2015
Finbar the Furious copyright © Paula Leyden 2015
Eleanor copyright © John Boyne 2015
Badness, Madness and Trickery copyright © Malachy Doyle 2015
The Beach of the Whispering Stones copyright © Maeve Friel 2015
The Princess who Wanted to be Queen copyright © Deirdre Sullivan 2015
The Sky-Snake and the Pot of Gold copyright © Darragh Martin 2015
Illustrations copyright © Olwyn Whelan 2015

First published in Great Britain and in the USA in 2015 by
Frances Lincoln Children's Books,
74-77 White Lion Street, London N1 9PF
QuartoKnows.com
Visit our blogs at QuartoKnows.com

This first paperback edition published in 2016

A catalogue record for this book is available from the British Library.

ISBN 978-1-84780-763-2

Illustrated with watercolours

Printed in China

1 3 5 7 9 8 6 4 2

MAGIC!

New Fairy Tales by Irish Writers

Edited by
Siobhán Parkinson

Illustrated by
Olwyn Whelan

Frances Lincoln
Children's Books

Contents

ear reader,

Ireland is a magic kind of place and it is full to bursting with stories and storytellers and writers. This book is your chance to get a sprinkling of Irish storytelling magic and also to discover some of our best Irish writers for children.

If there is one thing children (and even some adults) love to read, it's a good fairy tale, and we all love the old favourites. But even better than a familiar story that you love to read over and over again is a totally NEW fairy tale. Stories that use all the familiar things you love to read about (castles and forests and rainbows and baskets of food and promises and journeys and crowns and spells and wishes) but that are also fresh and new and take unexpected turns — these are hard to come by.

So I asked a terrific bunch of Irish children's writers to make up some new fairy tales to amaze, delight and amuse you. We've got well-known Irish writers in here (such as John Boyne) along with one or two you may be discovering in this book for the first time (such as Deirdre Sullivan and Darragh Martin). We have men (Malachy Doyle, for example) and women (me!), writers living in Ireland (Paula Leyden) and Irish writers living out of Ireland (Maeve Friel, for example), older writers and younger ones (no, we're not telling you — that's a secret). And we have a fantastic artist, Olwyn Whelan, to make the book absolutely sumptuous and gorgeous and magnificent — as you can see!

Some of the stories in this book are very funny. Some are just a wee bit sad in places or a teeny bit scary. (Leave the light on!) All of them are adventurous. And they all have great endings that will make you smile. And, of course, they are all absolutely MAGIC!

I hope you enjoy reading them as much as we have all enjoyed writing them. (Olwyn loved painting them too. She asked me to put that bit in.)
Happy fairy-tale reading!

Siobhán Parkinson

The Princess and the Other Frog

Siobhán Parkinson

Long, long ago, and a very long time it was, when there were still forests in Ireland, the Princess Finola set out to walk to The Other Side.

In those days, a princess could walk through a forest with only a pet frog for company. But of course she had to go in disguise. Because even in those days, there were people (and wolves and dragons and quite possibly ogres) who might make mischief if they thought that the little girl trotting through the woods with a picnic basket on her arm was actually a Princess of the Blood Royal.

My lovely red silk cape, the princess thought to herself, *with the lovely red silk hood. That's what I'll wear. People will think I'm That Other Girl.*

"Now, do you remember," asked her mother, wrapping up some oyster sandwiches and popping a bottle of peach juice into Finola's basket, "what you have to take to His Majesty, your Royal Father?"

"A rainbow's shadow," said the princess. "A silver lining. And a moon shower."

"And where will you meet His Majesty?" asked the queen.

"On The Other Side," said Finola. "But first I get to have my lunch."

"First you get to gather those things for His Majesty your Royal Father," said the queen.

After lunch, thought Finola. (She didn't know it was only oyster sandwiches. She was expecting crisps and chocolate, like other children get in their picnic baskets.)

So that was how the Princess Finola of the Blood Royal came to meet the Big Bad Wolf in the forest.

"God with you, girleen," said the Big Bad Wolf with a bow and a yellow smile and a sweep of his Big Bad Tail. "And what, pray, have you inside in your pretty little basket?"

Thinking it was crisps and chocolate and not wanting to share, the princess replied, "A rainbow's shadow."

"Musha!" cried the Big Bad Wolf. "That's the very thing I've been looking for myself for many a long day. May I take a look?"

"Certainly, noble sir," said the princess slyly. But instead of opening her basket, she caught hold of her pet frog, Hildegard by name, who was hidden inside her red silk cape, and flung her in the wolf's face, right in front of his Big Bad Fangs.

The Big Bad Wolf reeled back in surprise and snapped his Big Bad Wolfish jaws at the frog, but the frog, Hildegard by name, was too hoppity for him.

While all this was going on, the princess went sauntering on through the forest. Pretty soon the frog caught up with her mistress and hopped back into the secret pocket on the inside of Finola's lovely red silk cape.

Pretty soon after that, slithering and snorting along the forest floor, came a Fiery Red Dragon.

"God with you, my treasure," he snorted.

Finola was surprised to see him, but she didn't let on.

"And what, pray, have you inside in your pretty little basket?" asked the Fiery Red Dragon in a voice like bellows.

"A silver lining," answered Finola, thinking again about her crisps and chocolate.

"You don't say!" snorted the dragon. "The very thing I'm after. Could I take a peekeen of a look, do you think?"

"Indeed you could, noble sir," said Finola, and her pet frog, Hildegard by name, came leaping out from under the lovely red silk cape and leapt at the dragon.

There was a distinct aroma of singed frog in the air as the Princess Finola of the Blood Royal sauntered along, on her way to The Other Side of the forest. But pretty soon the pet frog, Hildegard by name, came limping along, smoking very slightly, and snuggled back inside Finola's cape.

Princess Finola was hungry by now, and was just about to open the picnic basket and take out a chocolate bar (as she thought), when who should come thundering and chundering and lurching and splurching through the forest but an Ogre.

"God with you, my little golden goose," roared the Ogre from a great height, so that his voice seemed to come from above the clouds and arrived in Finola's ears as if through a giant hearing-trumpet. "Pulse of my heart," he added, in case Finola didn't like being called a goose (which she did not). "And what, pray, have you inside in your pretty little basket?"

Finola was tempted to say 'Crisps and chocolate and you are not having any', but instead she said sweetly, "A moon shower."

"A moon shower?" yelled the Ogre. "My goodness gracious, the very thing I've been on the hunt for. Could I take a small lookeen?"

Finola said, "Certainly, noble sir," and made to open the top of her picnic basket.

The pet frog, Hildegard by name, in spite of one or two painful burns on her froggy little snout, came leaping out from under Finola's cape and leapt at the Ogre. But the Ogre was far too big to be fazed by a little scut of a frog, and he lifted his great Ogrish gallumph of a foot to squash her.

Finola gasped, grabbed the frog, stuffed her into her cape, scarpered through the forest, pell-mell, helter-skelter, like the clappers, all the way to The Other Side. And there to meet her was His Majesty, her Royal Father, splendid in crown and gown.

"God with you, bright love of my heart," he said. "And what have you got for me inside in your pretty little basket?"

Finola knew that all she had in her basket were crisps and chocolate and a bottle of something fizzy, but she said, "A rainbow's shadow, a silver lining and a moon shower, Your Majesty."

"The very things I wanted," said her father with a beam. And he never even looked in the basket! He handed it off to some underling, who took it home to his family that evening for supper, and they were surprised and delighted to find it contained (slightly toasted) oyster sandwiches and a bottle of peach juice.

"Father," said Finola, "there is someone I would like you to meet, Hildegard by name."

"What a noble name!" cried His Majesty. "Bring her forth, and I will kiss her for your sake."

The Princess Finola of the Blood Royal reached into her red silk cape and brought out the smoky and exhausted little pet frog, Hildegard by name.

You can guess what happened when the king kissed the frog, but that's another story. Let's just say the queen was not best pleased.

Finbar the Furious
The ogre who could do no wrong

Paula Leyden

On a sunny evening in June, in the year two thousand and thirteen, a child was born deep in the Tomnafinnoge forest in the Wicklow hills. This was no ordinary child, mind you, he was the first ogre born in Ireland since the Day of the Flaming Ogre Curse twelve hundred years before.

His proud parents took one look at him and named him Finbar the Furious. He had arrived into the world with a fearsome scowl on his ugly little face. Word spread throughout the land and ancient ogres travelled through hills and vales to come and view the miracle baby. They were, one and all, mightily pleased with what they saw.

Finbar the Furious had a head of wild and scraggy yellow hair, and the beginnings of what would turn into a most superior bushy beard. When he opened his mouth to spit at the visitors they saw, to their delight, a set of crooked rotten teeth as vile as any seen before. As his mother showed him off to the assembled hordes, she pointed to his finest feature, a pair of ears as lumpy as a bowl of cold oatmeal porridge.

They all agreed that Finbar the Furious was sure to grow up into a fine, monstrous ogre.

He grew quickly, as ogres do, and his parents watched as his hair grew longer and woollier, his beard sprouted and a few of his teeth fell out. Ogres, unlike children and sharks, do not grow a second set of teeth or even a third. He looked a picture.

But all was not as it should be. Finbar seemed to be lacking a certain something; he was perhaps not quite as furious as they had hoped he would be. When he was left to his own devices, Finbar was inclined to build things rather than knock them down. If stray deer or small hairy goats crossed his path, Finbar patted them gently if he thought no one could see him. However, when he knew his parents were watching, he would grunt and roar in proper ogre style, spitting and farting as he knew he should.

Finbar's parents weren't fooled.

One evening they hid behind a hill and watched as Finbar came upon a small piebald pony stuck in a ditch. As he came closer the little pony whinnied and harrumphed in terror, as you would if you were stuck in a ditch and Finbar the Furious was coming towards you. He leant down and quickly undid the barbed wire that had tangled around the little pony's legs.

His parents watched as he picked up the pony in his huge hands and held her close, all the while whistling in a tuneless manner. Tuneless it might have been, but the pony settled down, and to their amazement they saw her eyes close and her head drop. She fell fast asleep in the palm of his hand.

A huge smile spread across Finbar's big beardy face and a large tear splashed down from the corner of his eye.

His parents looked at one another. Both of them knew that there was nothing they could do. Their beloved son was never going to become a proper ogre.

They came out from their hiding place, and when Finbar saw them he slipped the little pony into his pocket and started picking his nose and burping loudly. He was very good at pretending.

His father stopped him with a roar. "All right, Finbar, enough with the burping! You don't even do it very well. We know you're not furious."

Finbar stopped.

"And that's all right. We still love you, even if you are kind to ponies and those hairy little goats." He gave a small shudder. "You started off so well. Ruder than all the rest, fouler than the foulest of them."

Finbar stood completely still with his hands in his pockets, one hand stroking the little pony in case his father's roaring was frightening her.

"But none of that matters," his mother added, in a roar that was even louder than his father's, "because you are still our very own ugly little Finbar the Furious — even if you're not very furious at all. We can still call you that, can't we?"

Finbar nodded. And just to make sure they believed him he put on a most hideous grimace and spat at them.

They smiled happily at one another as they wiped their faces.

Then they turned and stomped away towards the forest where they had a hard day's work ahead of them – frightening crows and laughing at donkeys.

Finbar put his hand back in his pocket and gently lifted the little pony out. He raised her up to his face and the tiny creature rubbed her soft nose against his.

Finbar the Furious, the ogre who could do no wrong, was now happy. He had made a new friend and he didn't have to pretend to be anything or anyone else ever again.

Eleanor

John Boyne

A queen gave birth to triplet sons, and such was the confusion in the castle that all three boys were placed in similar baskets so no one knew who had been born first.

A dispute broke out as to who would one day succeed to the throne and the king declared that as the boys grew, the true successor would display the qualities that all great rulers needed: an understanding of history, great skill on the battlefield and wise, calm judgement.

The boys were named Finian, Luke and Samuel and, as the years passed, their parents began to despair.

Finian was a hopeless scholar, unable to remember the names of the kings and queens who had preceded his parents. But there was not a man to be found who was more proficient in the jousting lists than he, nor was there anyone who could fell a deer with a single arrow from such great distances.

Luke could not sit atop a horse without falling off and had to be tied to his saddle when he went riding. But he wrote a magnificent history of the country, its rulers and subjects, its wars and treaties, and this made him a great favourite with the scholars of the land.

Samuel was known for his laziness, for he would rarely rise from his bed before lunchtime. But he had a pleasing disposition and a wisdom so respected that disputes were brought to him, and the decisions he made ensured that neighbours who had been in conflict returned to their homes arm in arm, resolving never to fight again.

"If only I had a son who combined the talents of all three!" cried the king, slumped on his throne in despair. "When I'm gone, my kingdom will be torn apart. My father had such a son — why don't I?"

A month later, a wealthy merchant from another land visited the castle, bringing chests filled with spices and exotic teas, precious jewels and robes, which he offered as gifts.

"You are most kind," said the king. "Your family must be among the greatest.

"Alas, sire," replied the merchant. "My wife is dead and my daughter still unmarried.

Distant relatives will fight over my estate when I am gone, for while my daughter is kind and affectionate, she has no mind for commerce."

The queen sought out the king later that same evening. "Might not Samuel be a good husband for the merchant's daughter?" she suggested. "He has intelligence and were they to be married, he would inherit that business and an enormous fortune."

"But the throne?" asked the king.

"We have two other sons," replied the queen.

The king agreed and an invitation was extended to the merchant's daughter to visit the castle, where the two young people were introduced. They fell in love and Samuel renounced the throne, happy to learn everything about his new business with his wife by his side.

Towards the end of the year, the chancellor of the university came to see the king and expressed his concern for the young, particularly now that he was close to retirement.

"The professors are an idle lot," he said. "Where will we be in fifty years if our young men do not have better teachers?"

"Might not Luke be a wise choice to run the university?" asked the queen, as she sat with the king over dinner. "There is no one with more knowledge of our past or a clearer insight into the mistakes and triumphs of previous rulers."

"But the throne?" asked the king.

"There's still Finian," replied the queen.

The king was uncertain, but he asked Luke whether the position might appeal to him. A lifetime of study and reading, of writing the great chronicles that the land needed? The boy could not believe his luck. And so, when the chancellor retired, Luke took his place in the university and renounced the throne for a lifetime of scholarship.

Across the water, words of war were being waged and the people worried that they would be invaded. "We need new blood at the head of the army," the soldiers told the king. "Someone we respect but who will be feared abroad."

"Might not Finian be the best person to lead the army?" asked the queen. "The soldiers love him and there is no more athletic man in the land."

"But the throne?" asked the king.

"There will be no throne if our neighbours invade," she replied. "If we are ever threatened, I can think of no one better suited to defending us."

The king agreed and put the proposition to his son. He had dreaded the idea of a lifetime spent within a castle, and he gladly renounced the throne in favour of spending his days marshalling the troops and seeing off invading armies.

"My health grows poor," moaned the king as winter approached. "I fear I will not see the spring. And our throne lies empty. Our sons are gone."

"But we have a daughter," said the queen, looking down towards the grounds of the castle where their fourth child, Eleanor, had left aside her study books to sprint across the fields to where two farm boys were fighting. She watched as the princess spoke to both and then, a moment later, the boys shook hands and were reconciled.

The king raised an eyebrow. Had this been part of the queen's plan all along? He had little doubt that it had for she had long believed that princes should not earn a kingdom simply by virtue of their gender.

And when his prophecy came true and he did not live to see the new leaves blossom on the trees, the princes Finian, Luke and Samuel returned to the castle to see their sister crowned queen. As Eleanor rose from her throne, the brothers kneeled before her to pledge their allegiance, and a great shaft of light shone down from the dome above, illuminating her robes as she looked out at her people with an expression of serenity that filled them with confidence.

The land thrived for sixty years after that. Through the association with the merchant's family, money flowed into the coffers and the people had work. The students graduating from the university were of the highest intelligence and passed their learning on to the generations that followed. And the land was kept safe from invasion by the bravery and fearlessness of the army.

The old queen went to her grave knowing that she had succeeded in the most important job of her life: choosing a worthy ruler for the kingdom.

Badness, Madness and Trickery

Malachy Doyle

Red weather nights, if the moon's shining bright and the wind's in the right direction, you'll maybe see them. Playing games in the back field, they'll be. They disappear as soon as you try and go near, of course.

Most people say it's just a trick of the light — but I know better, for I've seen them, oh yes. And not only that but I've met one too.

Way past my bedtime it was, and me on the way home from my friend, Joe Doherty's. We'd been kicking a football around out in the back field, and never even noticed how late it was.

I was wandering back by the light of the moon, and there he was, this tiny wee fellow, sitting on a wall, knitting a pair of multi-coloured socks and watching the world go by.

"How are you doing, young Michael McCarthy?" says he, laughing.

"Fine," says I. "Fine, indeed," not wishing to show my surprise, of course. My amazement, to tell you the truth, for seeing them's one thing, but talking to them's a whole different bag of bananas.

So we got to chatting about this and that, me pretending there was nothing at all odd about passing the time of day, late on a summer evening, with a wee fellow no bigger than your arm. Pretending, too, that I'd all the time in the world to be talking, when I knew, without a shadow of a doubt, that my poor old mother would be up the wall with worry.

He put down his knitting and pulled out his pipe for a smoke, and it was a tiny dainty thing, with the prettiest little carvings on it. He passed me his walking stick then, and I marvelled at the beauty of the workmanship.

So I showed him my penknife, opening out the blade and all, and he nearly fell to the ground in horror at the sheer size of the thing.

But the one thing I was trying to be extra-careful not to do, is to draw attention to his very own size. Because they're awful self-conscious of their littleness, or so I've heard the old people say, those that know a thing or two about such things. Yes, if you even so much as mention it you'd best be on your guard, for it turns them to badness – badness, madness or trickery!

But you know how it is. If there's one thing you're not supposed to mention, like the hairs on your granny's chin, then it's the one thing you find yourself saying. Or that's how it is with me, anyway.

So there's me, chatting away with your man like we're friends for life, when suddenly it slips out, all unawares.

"You know, it's a wonderful thing to be meeting you, sir," says I, "for you're the smallest wee man I've ever seen."

And as soon as I say it, I know I shouldn't have.

"Is it small you want?" says he, the colour rising in his face. "Look behind you, you great lumpen boychild, and you'll see one smaller still!"

So I did, and I didn't.

Yes, I looked and I looked, hoping to see an even tinier fellow than the one I'd just been talking to. And I thought I maybe heard a little squeaking, like you'd hear from a nest of fieldmice.

But not a soul could I see, though I'm down on my knees and crawling through the grass in the darkening light. Yes, I'm up to my eyes in cowpats, and not a thing to show for it but the muck and the odour.

For this other one he'd sent me to look for was a wee fellow, if fellow he was at all, so teeny-tiny-tinchy that I hadn't a hope in heaven of making him out. Sure, all I can hear is a high-pitched giggling from somewhere around or behind me.

"I can't see him anywhere," says I, turning back to your man, the one I was on about before.

And it was only then I realised it was all a badness and a madness, a trick and a tease! It was all about him getting his own back at me for doing the one thing I wasn't supposed to do – saying he was small.

For he'd gone. Vanished. Gone, and nothing but a half-finished sock and some tiny balls of wool to show he'd ever been there on the wall, talking away to me.

Gone, and my penknife with him!
Oh, the badness, the madness and
the little-people trickery!

The Beach of the Whispering Stones

Maeve Friel

 here once was a girl who lived out of a suitcase. She spent one week here, one week there, always packing and unpacking, always in trouble because she had left her toothbrush or her best trousers or her school library book in the wrong place. In both places, there were new babies. Everybody but the girl loved the new babies.

One night, when the moon was just a sliver of silver light and everyone was sleeping, the girl ran away. She didn't take her suitcase.

She ran across the dangerous road, past the leaning graveyard and the lake where the angry swans guarded their nests. When she turned down the lane to the strand and looked back, no one was coming after her.

She ran on.

The sea was black, rolling over the flat stones that gave the beach its name, *Trá Clocha na gCogar*, the Beach of the Whispering Stones. The girl picked one up and held it against her cheek.

Where the tide had turned, there was a straggle of seaweed. Mixed up with the tangles of plastic netting, cork floats and razor shells, there was a dead bird with oil-smeared feathers and its eyes pecked out.

She ran on.

Beside the rock pools, there was a rotting-fish smell and a dark black thing, half-in and half-out of the water. She looked back over her shoulder at the lights of the village and at the empty strand. No one was following her. The black thing was a seal with a bullet hole in its neck. The fishermen shot them, blaming the seals for breaking into their mussel beds.

I hate this place, the girl thought.

She ran on.

At the far end of the strand beyond the dunes, there was an outcrop of red rock. A woman was sitting on the very top, looking out to sea. Her long white hair reached down to her waist and her legs — if she had any — were tucked under her silvery speckly skirt. She was holding something close to her face, moving it up and down her cheek, most probably one of those whispering sea-smoothed stones.

She must be a mermaid, the girl thought, *listening to the songs of her mermaid family under the sea.*

She was careful not to frighten the woman away. She slipped behind the rock, took off her shoes and tiptoed, barefoot, to the water's edge.

The sea folded around her like a cold blanket. Silent as a clam, she lay face down, allowing her hair to flow out behind her, and scrabbled across the underwater reef with her hands until she reached the deeper water.

The girl was a good swimmer. She had badges that her mother sewed on to her tracksuit each time she reached a new personal record: 100m, 500m, 1000m, 2000m. Once on a charity swim, her father had ordered her out of the pool when she was still doing lengths long after everyone else had given up.

She could have gone on for ever.

She dived under, swam a few strokes, flipped over and floated on her back. A low black cloud scudded across the moon, blotting out the whole wide world, then cleared off, revealing the misty apparition of the mermaid on her rock, stroking her cheek with the smooth whispering stone.

She looks so sad, the girl thought. *She doesn't know where she belongs any more. She can't decide between her life on earth and her lost kingdom beneath the waves.*

She pinched her nose and dived down with a strong kick. The splash sent up a spray of phosphorescent lights which made the mermaid on her rock turn and frown.

The girl dived even deeper, startling a shoal of tiny silver fishes that turned tail and darted away. Even though her lungs were bursting, she kept on kicking, plunging towards the sea bed. She swam through a forest of waving sea-wrack with the bubbles that some called mermaids' purses and others called the devil's bladder.

She put her flat stone to her ear. "Come down, come down," she whispered to the mermaid. "This is a magical place. We two could live here in the sea together, away from all the cross people."

Far far away, there were bells ringing, urgent bells, and a loud wail.

"Come up, come up, my faerie child," the mermaid whispered back. "Come out of your lonely watery cave. There will be nothing but weeping and sadness if you stay there."

All around her, the waving seaweeds wrapped their branches around the girl and pulled her further into the watery forest.

"Come back, come back," the mermaid insisted. "It's not too late. Come back now."

The girl's ears popped. She pushed the water away from her and swam up, and up and up. When she broke the surface, sobbing and spluttering, she was blinded by the lights of the ambulance and the wailing police car and the flashing torches of all the people running over the flat stones of the whispering beach, looking for her. A lady in a long silvery dress was standing in the foam at the water's edge. She waded in and wrapped the girl in her arms.

"I was only swimming," the girl said, "swimming in the dark. But I heard a mermaid whispering."

The lady laid her cheek-warmed phone against the girl's cold back and rocked her. "I'm glad you heard her. This is where you belong."

The Princess who Wanted to be Queen

Deirdre Sullivan

nce upon a time there was a princess who made a deal with the Prince of Darkness. She only did it because she was sick of being told what to do. And also because the prince lived close by, in an enormous cottage that used to be a pub that he had won in a game of cards. Which is a pretty handy way to get a house. All he'd needed to change was the roof, because the thatch kept going on fire whenever he sneezed.

What the princess really wanted, more than anything, was to be the queen after her father died and was done being king. In her kingdom, you weren't allowed to be a queen until you had a king to help you be the boss of things. Getting married meant you had to wear a white dress and hang out with a man all day long, and probably after the wedding was over as well.

The Prince of Darkness was tall and smelled of turf smoke. He had hairy legs and long thin fingers like a piano player. He was terrifying, but also charming.

The princess knocked at the prince's heavy black door. The knocker was red as tongues and shaped like a Bengal tiger.

"What can I do for you?" the prince asked. He liked to get right to the point so he didn't have to spend all day talking to people about weather and their health. The Prince of Darkness didn't care how the weather was unless there was a storm with sheet lightning.

Now, the prince had a lot of souls, but he was always after more. He put them in glass jars and kept them on shelves in a special room that looked dark to everybody else but glowed to him so brightly. He wanted the princess's soul because it was a pleasant combination of lilac and lapis lazuli. He could tell right away that she would be an amazing ruler.

"I hear you're in the soul-collecting business," said the princess.

"Where did you hear that?" asked the prince.

"From people whose souls you collected," said the princess.

"Fair enough," said the prince.

"Would you like to lease my soul for a while?" offered the princess. "I'm not really prepared to let you have it full-term, because I'll probably need it to get into heaven."

"I don't lease souls," replied the prince. His nostrils flared and he stroked the ridiculous little beard that was shaped like a triangle balancing on his chin.

"I know you don't ordinarily. But I'm royal and do LOADS of charity work, so I thought that you might be willing to make an exception. You could pretend I'd won it back through some sort of clever trickery. Like that man in Kerry did a few years ago."

"You heard about that one, did you?" said the prince. Everyone had heard about that blasted Kerryman, and it really annoyed the prince.

"I did," said the princess.

"Hmmm," said the Prince of Darkness, making a triangle shape out of his fingers. "What would you want in return?"

The prince was very interested in the things that people wanted. If you don't know what someone wants it is really hard to corrupt them.

"Well, people say I have to marry in order to become queen, but I don't want to," said the princess. "And my dad says he wants to meet his grandchildren before he dies. I'm not even sure I want to have children. They're kind of noisy. Though Dad says they're not actually all that noisy and I'd probably like them once I got to know them."

"But you're not convinced."

"I want to spend my first few years of ruling the kingdom actually ruling the kingdom. And what if I married someone who thought he could boss me around?"

"But are you sure you want to give me your soul instead? You'd have to go to hell."

"Not if it's only on lease."

The prince looked at the princess. He didn't want to put her soul in a jar and look at it in a dark room full of souls. He wanted to keep looking at it flowing and ebbing around the smooth curves of her body. He wanted to look at it as he listened to her baby-bear's porridge of a voice. Suddenly, an idea came to him.

"How about you marry me?"

"Are you even allowed to get married?" asked the princess. The prince seemed too swishy and flickery to be tied down by any one woman.

"I'm allowed to do anything I want," said the prince. "I am the Prince of Darkness and no creature is the boss of me. Also, it would be a pretty short-term thing. I'd probably abandon you after a while."

"So I wouldn't have to give you my soul?" said the princess.

"No."

"And is this some sort of mean trick?"

"Well, I am going to abandon you, so yes."

"But I don't want to be stuck with a forever husband, even one who smells as nice as you do."

"You think I smell nice?" The prince was pleased. This was a Good Sign.

"Yes," said the princess. "Yes, I do. All right, so I'll marry you for a year and a half and then review our contract. But I don't want you drunk with power, setting fire to things and starting wars. Not in my kingdom."

"Fair enough," said the prince and he started drawing up a contract with his tail. It was pretty impressive.

But as it turned out, the prince ended up staying with the princess for years and they had two fine sons and one fine daughter together, all with beautiful voices and souls, swishy tails and lovely smells and hairy little legs.

The Sky-Snake and the Pot of Gold

Darragh Martin

Nora had a lot of secrets for a small girl. Her first secret was that the hill she lived on was the very best one to roll down in the whole of Ancient Ireland. Every afternoon, Nora had a rolling-race with the squirrels and the hedgehogs.

Nora's second secret was that she was tall enough to climb out of her bedroom window. She did this when she played chasing with the owls and bats, who only visited at night.

But Nora's third secret was definitely the biggest.

If you have ever seen a sky-snake you will know that it really is a BIG secret. There aren't as many sky-snakes in the sky as there once were, but you can still see them if you spend enough time outside. They're especially fond of wet weather.

If you look up after it rains, you will probably see their bodies arched across the sky. Finding their heads is harder. Sky-snakes are shy enough. You need to have a good pair of eyes, a brave heart and a little bit of luck. Nora had all three and so she'd been friends with the sky-snake since she was four.

Nora liked all the creatures who shared the hill with her (especially when she beat them in a rolling-race) but the sky-snake was her best friend. This particular sky-snake was named Síle. Síle was brilliant. She let Nora ride on her back so that the ground was small below and Nora could taste the clouds. Sometimes Nora slid down her tail so that she landed back on her hill with a bump.

On Nora's birthdays, Síle turned over and let Nora bounce up and down on her belly. Some days, Nora and Síle just curled up side by side on the hill and shared stories. Síle had lots of tales about the wide world that she stretched over, and Nora loved making up stories about the small hill that she knew so well.

The trouble started one rainy Monday morning.

As soon as Nora saw the Golden Gang zoom up to her hill in their golden chariots, she knew that the sky-snake was no longer a secret. The Golden Gang were the richest children in Ancient Ireland. They lived in the hugest castle and had the shiniest clothes. They all had extra letters in their name because they liked to sound important.

"I see a sky-snake and I want my pot of gold," a boy named Conorrrr said that Monday morning.

The Golden Gang believed that sky-snakes marked the spot where incredible riches were buried. Every time they saw a sky-snake they dug up the ground below. Ancient Ireland was full of huge holes where they had torn up tree roots or nice mounds of grass.

"It's MY pot of gold!" Conorrrr's twin sister Aoiffffe screamed. "I need more gold to fuel my chariot!"

Nora coughed. She did not like the dirty golden smoke that rose out of the chariots. Or the huge jaws that opened at the front. Nora put her hands on her hips, the way her mother did when she was angry, and told the Golden Gang that they were not going to dig up her hill. And that her parents would be very angry when they got home.

"Get out of my way before I run you over!" Aoiffffe shouted.

The Golden Gang were not very good listeners. But they were good at digging. The huge jaws of their chariots reached hungrily for grass. The ladybirds quivered. The hedgehogs rolled into balls.

And then Nora had an idea.

If you have seen a sky-snake, you know that they have lots of coloured stripes. What you might not know is that sky-snakes are able to stretch their stripes. If they wanted to, they could make an entire hill seem one colour. Especially if a small girl they were fond of told them to.

The Golden Gang screamed as the whole hill turned bright red.

"Run away, run away," Nora said. "This isn't a hill. It's a GIANT VAMPIRE'S TONSIL! Run away before you're all munched up!"

The next morning, the Golden Gang came back with special suits made of garlic. So Síle stretched her stripes again – and the hill turned bright orange.

"Run away, run away," Nora said. "This isn't a hill. It's a DRAGON'S FIERY NOSTRIL! Run away before you're burnt to a crisp!"

The next morning, the Golden Gang came back with suits made out of hose-pipes. Síle stretched her stripes and the hill turned bright yellow.

"Run away, run away," Nora said. "This isn't a hill. It's a SUN'S BURNING EYEBALL! Run away before you're all blind as bats!"

The next morning, the Golden Gang came back with huge sunglasses. Síle sretched her stripes and the hill turned bright green.

"Run away, run away," Nora said. "This isn't a hill. It's a GIANT'S STICKY SNOT! Run away before you all get stuck!"

The next morning, the Golden Gang came back with very big tweezers. Síle stretched her stripes and the hill turned bright blue.

"Run away, run away," Nora said. "This isn't a hill. It's a BLUE WHALE'S BELLY! Run away before he wakes up!"

The next morning, the Golden Gang came back in a large submarine. Síle stretched her stripes and the hill turned violet.

"Run away, run away," Nora said. "This IS a hill. But it's INFESTED WITH BOUNCING BLACKBERRIES!"

Nora had been lucky that time. She was glad the ladybirds had bounced up and down for her. But the Golden Gang weren't all that scared of bouncing blackberries. They came back that night with a huge mallet to squash them. Nora climbed out of her window and ran over.

Síle had saved her sixth stripe for last. It was her smallest stripe. Some people said it was so small it wasn't even a colour. But sometimes small things can be very special.

And the truth was, this stripe was a little bit magic.

Nora looked at Síle's sixth stripe which was as dark and deep as the night sky. She knew that she didn't have to tell any stories. Her small voice stopped the giant mallet and the enormous jaws.

"Run away, run away," Nora said. "This is a hill but you can't dig it up. The squirrels love to climb that tree. The hedgehogs love the grass. And underneath that stone, there are all sorts of insects that have never lived anywhere else. This is our home. It's worth more than any gold for your chariots."

All the creatures who shared the hill stood beside Nora. The squirrels climbed on top of the chariot jaws. The hedgehogs rolled in front of the mallet. The tiniest insects bit at the chariot wheels so they had no air. Two sleepy parents stood beside their daughter, their pride as huge as the hill.

The Golden Gang didn't come back after that night. Neither did Síle. She didn't think it was safe for the hill. But she left a little piece of sky-snake behind on the hill. It was only a tiny patch of grass, in a colour so small most people couldn't see it. Nora could, though. She told her children about it. Then she told her grandchildren.

And she was still telling her great-grandchildren the same story many years later…

"When you see a sky-snake, don't bother about the pot of gold," she'd say. "Look for the pot of indigo instead. Because sometimes small things are the best. Sometimes creatures as small as yourselves can make a difference as huge as the sky."

About the Authors

John Boyne is the author of nine novels for adults and four for younger readers, including *The Boy in the Striped Pyjamas*, which was made into a Miramax feature film. His work is translated into over 45 languages. www.johnboyne.com

Malachy Doyle lives on a tiny island off the coast of Donegal with his wife Liz, two dogs, two cats and three ducks. He has written over one hundred books, for children of all ages. www.malachydoyle.com

Maeve Friel was born in Derry, Northern Ireland, and lived for many years in Spain. She died in September 2015. She was the author of several novels, chapter books, short stories and picture books. Her work has been translated into over twenty languages. www.maevefriel.com

Paula Leyden lived in Kenya, Zambia and South Africa before moving to Kilkenny, Ireland, where she now lives on a farm with her partner, their five children, six horses, two donkeys, three dogs and three cats. Her website is at www.thebutterflyheart.net where you can learn more about her books and her life.

Darragh Martin writes plays and children's books. His first novel for children, *The Keeper*, was published by Little Island in 2013 and was short-listed for an Irish Book Award.
www.darraghmartin.com

Siobhán Parkinson was Ireland's first laureate for children's literature. Her most recent books are *Alexandra*, for tinies, and the companion novels *Bruised* and *Heart-shaped*, for young teenagers. She lives in Dublin and runs a small publishing company, Little Island Books. She likes listening to audiobooks and looking at the sky.
www.siobhanparkinson.com

Deirdre Sullivan has written three YA novels, *Prim Improper, Improper Order* and *Primperfect*. Her next book, *Needlework,* will be released in 2016.
www.facebook.com/DeirdreSullivan/Writer

ALSO AVAILABLE FROM FRANCES LINCOLN CHILDREN'S BOOKS

Spellbound
Tales of Enchantment from Ancient Ireland
978-1-84780-459-4

Told for younger children by the first Irish Children's Laureate, with beautiful colour illustrations, are these seven magical stories from Ancient Ireland.

Butterfly Girl
The Enchanted Deer
Land Under Wave
The Children of Lir
The Enchanted Birds
Cú Chulainn and Emer
Labhra with the Horse's Ears

Shortlisted for the CBI Book of the Year Award 2013

'The perfect introduction to Irish folk tales'
– Books for Keeps

Frances Lincoln titles are available from all good bookshops.
You can also buy books and find out more about your favourite titles,
authors and illustrators on our website: www.franceslincoln.com